BOOK 5

SET OFF FIREWORKS

A LITTLE BOOK OF BIG CHOICES

RICKETY & RACKETY

BOOK 5

SET OFF FIREWORKS

D.Z. MAH

Printed in the United States of America

First Printing, 2021

ISBN: 978-1-953888-45-7

WorkHorse Productions, Inc.

Formatting by:

emtippettsbookdesigns.com

OTHER LITTLE BOOKS OF BIG CHOICES

Rickety and Rackety's Complete Fire Unsafety Collection

Math Pirates: The Complete Quest for the Pickled Pearl

Merfriends: The Complete Water Safety Collection

Mage Academy: The Complete Collection
(tests and trials)

The Adventures of Billy the Chimera Hunter
(safe and risky choices)

The Pippa the Werefox Mysteries Volume I
The Pippa the Werefox Mysteries Volume II
The Pippa the Werefox Mysteries Volume III

Learn more about us and get free ebooks at

littlebooksofbigchoices.com

A NOTE TO THE READER

Most cultures around the world have at least one holiday with fireworks. In the US it is the Fourth of July. In the UK it is Bonfire Night. In India it is Diwali. These holidays can be a lot of fun, but the fireworks mean they can also be very dangerous.

This book will teach you how to be safe, so that you can have more fun. The best holidays are holidays when nobody gets hurt.

One rule of firework safety is that younger children should not light fireworks. Always have an adult light the fuse, while you sit back and enjoy the show. And if you want to see big fireworks that shoot high into the sky, make sure to watch a show that is done by professionals. That can be the most fun way of all to watch fireworks.

FIREWORKS

You hear a crash in the other room and you and the raccoons look at each other through the window. Rickety and Rackety aren't allowed to come inside buildings with you. They say they want to be better about starting fires and did really well on the family camping trip. But now that you're all back in the city, they are back to their fire-starting ways.

Rackety is even holding a lighter in one paw as she peers in the window at you.

"What happened?" Rickety asks.

You're in an abandoned house, salvaging it for supplies. Your parents had you looking through the wrecked remains of a living room while they tackled the garage, which is where the crashing noise came from.

Crashing noises are not good, in your experience.

"Are you okay?" you call out.

"We're fine, honey," your mother replies. "We just found something."

From her tone of voice, you can't tell if it's a good or bad something, and the raccoons are clearly curious.

Well, you're curious too. The raccoons ignore the rules and come bounding inside.

They aren't allowed near the garage because that's the most common place people used to store things like gasoline. It's not a place for raccoons who like to play with fire.

"Stay there," you order your friends. You pick your way through the kitchen—which looks like it was hit by a tornado and has splintered wood all over the floor—and go to the dark garage, where your parents are both staring down into a cardboard box on the floor, their headlamps dropping little pools of light.

"What is it?" you ask.

They both look up at you, blinding you for a moment with their headlamps until they both push them up on their heads so that they light the ceiling instead of your eyes.

"Fireworks," says your father. "We found a box of old fireworks. They look like they're in really good condition, though."

"Really?" You've heard of fireworks, but never seen them. According to your parents, they used to be pretty common, but nowadays, no one really makes them anymore. "Can we set them off?"

Your parents look at each other, then your mother nods. "We'll set them off, but we're going to do it the right way. Safely, okay?"

You're not sure why your parents bother to say this. It's not as if you expected them to suddenly decide to be unsafe and put you in danger, but you nod in agreement anyway. Grown-ups are weird sometimes.

"Where are the raccoons?" Dad asks.

"Uh, knowing them," you say, "they'll be here any—"

"Hey!" Rickety comes bounding into the garage. "Is everything okay in here?"

You turn around just in time to see Rackety arrive, the lighter still clutched in her paw.

"Okay." You head for the exit. "We're all going outside right now."

"Rule one," says Dad, "only the grown-ups light the fireworks."

"Aw," says Rickety. "We've seen plenty of kids light fireworks."

"I'm sure you have," says Mom.

"Wait, what?" You look at your parents.

"Not everyone is safe with fireworks," says your father. "But we are going to be, all right? You can choose which ones to light, and you can help us find a good place to set them off."

"I reject rule one." Rickety folds his arms. "It's our lighter. We light the fireworks."

"We're adults," Rackety agrees. "We

finished growing years ago."

Your parents exchange a look, and you're afraid they'll just get rid of the fireworks. They hesitate, though.

"Fine," says Mom. "We set them up, and you can light them, but you have to follow all of our instructions."

Yes! you think.

The raccoons both dance around.

You head for outside. "Let's go!"

The five of you all walk through the house and out the front door. The house is at the end of a cul-de-sac and the road is still in good condition. There aren't any weeds growing through cracks in the asphalt.

However, you know this neighborhood doesn't have any running water. It was shut off when all the houses were declared abandoned.

You could also go back to your neighborhood where there is running water, but the street isn't as wide.

Where do you want to set off fireworks?

Your neighborhood (turn to page 11)

In the cul-de-sac (turn to page 36)

Now you know it's not a good idea to set off fireworks without a source of water nearby. You're back at the house with the unused box of fireworks. This time, you're taking them back to your neighborhood to light.

YOUR NEIGHBORHOOD

In this book, you live in a world where there is only running water in places where people live. None of the abandoned houses have running water. So, if you want to be near a faucet with water, you need to go to a place where there are people.

Water is probably important if you're lighting fireworks.

When you point this out to your parents, they agree. They load the fireworks and the rest of the day's salvage in the car and tell the raccoons to meet you at your house.

You're not sure how the raccoons travel as fast as they do, but they are waiting for you on your street when you arrive, and they are bouncing with excitement and waving the lit lighter in the air.

The sun set during the drive, so if it wasn't for the lighter, you would have trouble seeing the raccoons (Authors' Note: this isn't a good reason to have a lighter on a regular street where people live. There are better ways to be seen.)

Your parents park the car in the garage and then carry the fireworks out to the sidewalk.

"Okay," says your father. "Rule two, you don't go in the street. Only one raccoon and I go in the street to light fireworks, all right?"

You, Rickety, and Rackety nod.

Mom switches on her headlamp so that you can all look in the box of fireworks.

"I think we should be careful about fireworks that shoot too high or jump or fly," says your father. "So I'm thinking we should light these."

He pulls out a box of sparklers and a couple of bags of fireworks that claim to make flower shapes on the ground.

They aren't the most exciting fireworks in the box, but since you've never seen any fireworks, you're interested to try them.

Rickety and Rackety snatch them out of your parents' hands and look them over critically.

"Some of these have been damaged with water," says Rackety, holding up some of the ground flower fireworks.

"These don't do anything," says Rickety. "They just sparkle and you run around waving them."

"You do *not* run around," says Mom. "You hold them and watch them. They are pretty and fun."

Rickety gives your mother a doubtful look.

But both raccoons turn to look at you, curious to know which one you'll choose.

What firework do you want to light?

The sparklers (turn to page 16)

The ground flowers (turn to page 26)

You ended up not liking the ground flower fireworks much. They made you want to stop lighting fireworks altogether. But now you're back to when you've just arrived at your house, and this time, you're going to light the sparklers. Maybe those will be more fun.

SPARKLERS

The sparklers look like they could be fun, so you pull out the box and hand it to your mother.

Dad, meanwhile, fills a bucket of water and brings it over.

"Do we get sparklers?" the raccoons ask.

Your parents give them a doubtful look.

"Hey." You fold your arms. "They haven't

set anything on fire all day."

"That we know of," says Mom.

Your father sighs and hands each raccoon a sparkler.

"Some more rules," he says. "No running with the sparklers. No carrying them near anything that can burn. No waving them in people's faces."

"This is no fun," says Rickety.

You lean down and whisper, "Don't say that. You won't get to keep your sparkler."

Rickety's ears and tail droop, but he says, "I mean, I'm really glad we're being so safe."

"O-kay," says your father to you. "Hold your sparkler still until Rackety gets it lit. It takes a minute with sparklers."

Rackety lights the lighter and you hold the tip of your sparkler in its flame.

Dad is right. It does take a while for the

sparkler to light, but eventually it does in a white flash of twinkling sparks.

"Me, me!" says Rackety. She touches her sparkler to yours and a moment later it lights.

"Now me!" Rickety lights his sparkler on Rackety's

"Ooooh," both raccoons say, gazing in awe at the brilliant sparks flying everywhere.

You're not so sure this was a good idea. They love fire. You hope they don't go looking for other sparklers to light on their own. Maybe you should make sure to use up the whole box tonight.

The sparks drop off your sparkler onto the ground, where they wink out. It is pretty neat.

As the sparkler burns, the sparks move closer and closer to your hand, until they run out of fuel and the sparkler winks out.

"Quick," wails Rackety. "Light another one or else we have to use the lighter. She thrusts her sparkler at you.

You jump back before she can set your clothing on fire, and Mom gives her a warning look.

But Dad hands you another sparkler and you quickly touch it to Rackety's to light it.

You get yours lit just before Rackety's goes out.

"Mine'll go out next," Rickety wails.

Well, at least it won't be hard to go through all the sparklers. Your dad works frantically to keep handing them out so that you can light each other's.

Though, the sparklers get less and less interesting the longer you stand around holding one. It was cool to start with, but these fireworks don't really do much other than sparkle.

The raccoons are fascinated, though, gazing at the flying sparks with their beady little eyes.

Rackety walks over to a soda can lying discarded on the sidewalk and holds the sparkler to it. "I want to see if I can melt the metal!"

"No," you argue. "No way."

"Whoa..." She picks up the can and runs towards you with it.

"No running!" you, Mom, and Dad all shout.

Rackety slows down, but she's close enough to hold out the soda can to you. There's a big black mark on the side of it. "I melted it!" she announces.

"No, you didn't," argues Rickety.

"Did so!"

While they're talking, you squat down to

look at the can more closely, and accidentally touch your sparkler to your shoelace, which catches fire quickly.

"In the bucket!" Mom shouts.

You toss your sparkler into the water, where it fizzles out, and with your other foot you stamp out your burning shoelace.

With a frown, your father picks up the soda can. "There is a hole in it, here," he says.

"I told you I melted it!" Rackety crows, holding her sparkler aloft.

Dad gets out his phone, no doubt to look up whether she can be right.

You made good decisions here. Now are you ready to learn some surprising things about sparklers?

1.   Sparklers can burn as hot as 3000 degrees
      Fahrenheit (1600 degrees celsius). They
      may look very pretty, but they can also
      be quite dangerous.

2.   Yes, Rackety did melt a little hole in the
      drink can with her sparkler. Aluminum
      melts at 1200 degrees Fahrenheit. That
      should give you an idea of how hot
      sparklers are. They have a very small
      flame, though, and that is why the hole
      she made is so little.

3.   Sparklers can easily light clothing on fire.
      One common accident is sparks falling
      on your shoes and setting them on fire,
      like what happened when you squatted
      down.

4.   Although many people think of sparklers as a safe firework, you shouldn't give them to little kids to hold. Use safer items like glow sticks for them to play with. It is far too easy for them to burn themselves, someone else, or catch their clothing on fire.

5.   Always have that bucket of water handy, and yes, throw your sparkler in if anything goes wrong.

This book has four endings and each one will teach you something different about fireworks. If you haven't read all four, you can...

...go back one step and choose to light the ground flowers instead (turn to page 25),

go back two steps and choose to light fireworks in the cul-de-sac, even though there is no running water there (turn to page 35),

go back to the beginning and re-read the first scene (turn to page 3), or

if you've read all four endings, turn to page 58 for a final word from Rickety and Rackety.

Well, you've played with the sparklers, and that was more exciting than you wanted it to be. You're back at your house, and this time you're going to choose to light the ground flower fireworks instead.

GROUND FIREWORKS

The raccoons assure you that the fireworks called "ground flowers" are a lot of fun. You're not sure if that means it's a good idea to light them, but they stay on the ground, so how dangerous can they be?

"Those," you say, pointing.

Your dad opens the package, looks both ways, and then walks out into the middle of the street with Rickety on his heels to light them.

Once Dad has the fireworks set out how he wants them, he nods to Rickety.

Rickety lights the fuse and runs back to where you stand. You realize that standing next to a box of fireworks isn't a good idea, so you walk a little further down the sidewalk and the raccoons both follow you.

The fuse burns and burns, and then winks out.

All five of you continue to stare, waiting for the fireworks to do something.

They don't.

"Duds!" Rickety shouts. "They are duds!"

"It's all right," says Dad. He gets out some more and walks out into the street.

Rickety dashes out to light them.

This time, when he runs away from the lit fuse, he runs towards you. As soon as he reaches

27

you, the ground flowers ignite, spinning across the asphalt in bright colors and sending sparks shooting everywhere.

Well, most of them stay on the ground, that is. One of them sails into the air with a loud whistle and flies straight towards your neighbor's house, landing on the roof.

For a moment all you can do is stare as the spent firework rests there, burning slowly.

Then your dad is pelting across the street. "Becca! Marge! Get your hose!"

Fortunately, their sprinkler is already hooked up in the front yard. Your father tosses it onto the roof and then turns on the water.

Your neighbors come out of their house looking confused, and no doubt wondering why your father is using their sprinkler on the roof.

Since it's the kind of sprinkler that rotates

slowly, it doesn't put the fire out at once. It has to make a couple of passes, but it does finally work. You hope there isn't too much damage to their roof.

Just as you're starting to relax, more ground flowers ignite in the street, dancing around and spinning and sparking. Oh no, the raccoons are in trouble now.

Or... wait...

Both raccoons are with you. Neither of them went and lit any more fireworks. Those ground flowers are the first batch, the ones you thought were duds. They'd been quietly burning away while you were dealing with the neighbors' roof, and now they've gone off.

Rickety runs over and kicks at one, sending it flying towards Rackety.

"No!" your mother shouts.

Rickety darts back to the sidewalk, his

ears down. "I was just having fun."

"Never kick or throw a firework at anyone," Mom orders him. "Never touch a firework that is going off. You shouldn't even hold lit fireworks other than sparklers, okay?"

Rickety nods.

"You could've blinded me!" Rackety shrieks. "Or burned my fur off."

"She's right," you agree. "That was really dangerous."

It's not fun to watch fireworks anymore. You've had enough, and you tell your parents this.

"Can we have the rest of the fireworks?" Rackety asks.

"No," say both of your parents at the same time.

Dad is busy pulling the sprinkler down off the roof.

Mom packs up the fireworks and says to the raccoons, "If I catch either of you so much as touching this, you can never spend time with us again.

You expect the raccoons to laugh at that, but their ears droop and they look truly sad.

"Okay," says Rickety. "We'll leave them alone."

You made good choices here, but as I'm sure you've figured out, fireworks are still dangerous even if you make good choices. What did you learn this time?

1.   Always have that bucket of water handy when you're lighting fireworks. It doesn't hurt to have a hose hooked up as well.

2.   Put dud fireworks into the bucket of water. Never assume that because they didn't go off when you lit them that they will never go off. They are still full of all kinds of material that burns very hot and very fast.

3.   Fireworks landing on roofs is actually a pretty common fire hazard. This is why setting off fireworks near anyone's house can be dangerous. Be ready with a hose— or even better, don't set off fireworks near people's houses if you can avoid it.

4.   Fireworks are unpredictable. Even if they were made to stay on the ground, there's

always a chance one could go flying. Always be on your guard near fireworks.

5. Never ever pick up a lit firework. You also shouldn't kick it or throw it, and you especially should not kick or throw it at someone else.

There are four endings to this story, and each one should teach you something different about fireworks. If you haven't read all four endings, you can...

...go back one step and choose to light the sparklers instead (turn to page 15),

go back two steps and light fireworks in the cul-de-sac, away from people's houses (but remember there's no water out there) (turn to page 35),

go back to the beginning and re-read the first scene (turn to page 3), or

if you've read all four endings, turn to page 58 for a final word from Rickety and Rackety.

You're back at the house you've been salvaging with your parents, and this time, you're going to choose to light fireworks there, in the cul-de-sac. There's no water source, but you've got a good, flat area of road that is far away from anything that can burn.

IN THE CUL-DE-SAC

Y ou like how big and wide the street is here at the end of the cul-de-sac. "Is this a good place to set off fireworks?" you ask.

"I think so," says your father. "It's far away from any of the houses."

"All right!" you say.

Your parents carry the fireworks out to

the middle of the street and pick out ones to set off.

The day was warm enough that you can smell the tar in the asphalt and the raccoons complain as they scamper along that it's hot under their paws.

It's getting dark, though, which is good. That's the time to set off fireworks, you hear.

By the time you reach your parents, they have two options for you to choose from.

One firework looks like a cone and says it's a fountain. It says it shoots sparks up to ten feet in the air. You look around and are pretty sure you're more than ten feet from the curb.

Another firework is called a bottle rocket because it is supposed to be put in a bottle or can and will fly up into the air once it's lit. But you don't have a bottle or can.

"We can just stick it in this crack in the

asphalt," your father reasons. "That'll hold it in the right position before it takes off."

They both look like a lot of fun.

The raccoons pick up the fireworks in their paws and examine them carefully.

"Have you ever seen either of these lit?" you ask.

"Mmm-hmm," says Rackety, turning the bottle rocket over in her paws. "This one's in good condition. The fountain looks like it's been sitting around a while."

"What happens when they sit around a while?" you ask.

"I don't know," says Rackety. "We tried to light some once that had a lot of water damage, and they were all just duds. They didn't do anything. This fountain just looks old. It doesn't look like it's ever been wet."

The two raccoons put the fireworks

down and shrug. They don't care which one you decide to light first.

Which one do you want to light first?

The bottle rocket (turn to page 41)

The fountain (turn to page 49)

You're back in the cul-de-sac, picking which firework to set off. You already know that the fountain worked well and not to sit close to the box of fireworks. This time you're going to be a little more daring and choose to set off the bottle rocket.

A BOTTLE ROCKET
WITHOUT A BOTTLE

Surely your dad knows what he's doing. You help him stick the bottle rocket in the crack in the asphalt while Mom carries the box of fireworks over to the sidewalk. You and Rackety stay away from that box as you go to a different section of sidewalk and sit down. The concrete is still warm from the day, but won't be for long. You can tell it's cooling fast.

Rickety flicks the lighter on and holds the flame against the fuse of the bottle rocket, then runs towards you once the fuse is on fire.

A jet of flame shoots out from the bottom of the bottle rocket, knocking it sideways.

It is pointing straight at you.

You and the raccoons run for cover as the firework shoots right at the place where you were just sitting. It slams into the house behind you and sends beautiful, colored sparks in all directions.

You get lucky, though. The house is brick, and the firework falls harmlessly onto the concrete patio. There are sure to be scorch marks, but nothing catches fire.

"Sooo," says Rickety. "Why didn't you use a bottle?"

"We don't have any bottles." You shrug.

"Oh, there are a whole bunch of bottles in

.Z. MAH

the backyard of that house you were salvaging."

"Why didn't you say so before?" you ask. Honestly, you don't understand your raccoon friends sometimes.

"You didn't ask." His voice is fading because as he says this, he is already running for the yard. A moment later he returns with a glass soda bottle and holds it up. "Use this!"

Your father gives him a sheepish smile. "Yes, we should do that."

He takes the bottle and sets it in the middle of the cul-de-sac, then places another bottle rocket in it.

You and Rackety again sit on the curb, but you are ready to get up and run if you have to.

Rickety lights the fuse and runs towards you.

This time the bottle rocket shoots up into

43

the sky and explodes in a whistling shower of colored sparks. You and the raccoons applaud.

"That is awesome!" says Rackety.

"Light another one," says Rickety.

So your father goes back out to the bottle, places another bottle rocket in it, and lets Rickety light it.

And as he's backing away, the bottle falls over. This time it points the bottle rocket at a different house, which isn't near anyone, at least.

The bottle rocket fires straight into the front door, then bounces off onto the lawn, then explodes with a loud bang and a shower of sparks.

The house catches fire in several spots as hot sparks land on its exposed wood.

"Water!" shouts Rickety. "We've got to find water!"

You already know there isn't any water, though, and now the fire's getting bigger, consuming the wood around the house's front windows.

Dad shuts his eyes a moment, then pulls out his phone and calls the fire department.

You made a decision you don't want to make in real life (but is just fine to make in a book) and a house is now on fire. What did you learn? You should have learned:

1. Bottle rockets are a dangerous firework. All fireworks are dangerous, but flying fireworks like bottle rockets are extra dangerous. They are illegal in a lot of

places for a good reason. It is better to go watch a fireworks show put on by professionals than to play with bottle rockets. At a show, you will see even bigger fireworks and it will be safer.

2. When a firework comes with directions, like to put it in a bottle, follow the directions. Don't try to do something different, like sticking it in the ground.

3. Even when you do follow the directions on a bottle rocket, it can still misfire, so be careful no matter what.

4. Always have a bucket of water around when you're lighting fireworks. You need it to put out fires, and also to soak used fireworks before throwing them away.

There are four endings to this story, and each one will teach you something different about fireworks. If you haven't read all four endings, you can...

...go back one step and choose to light the fountain (turn to page 48),

go back two steps and choose to take the fireworks back to your street, where there is running water (turn to page 10),

go back to the beginning and re-read the first scene (turn to page 3), or

if you've read all four endings, turn to page 58 for a final word from Rickety and Rackety.

The bottle rockets didn't turn out so great. You're back in the cul-de-sac, picking which firework to light. This time, you're going with the fountain.

A FOUNTAIN FIREWORK

Since you're more than ten feet away from the curb, it seems like a fountain that only goes ten feet in the air is a good choice. This way, if it falls over, it won't set anything on fire.

The problem is that it's old. The label is faded, and it looks like it's been sitting around a long time.

Still, this is the firework you hold out to your parents.

Your mother sets it down in the street and beckons to Rickety.

Rackety carries the box of fireworks away, and your father watches her carefully, afraid that she'll run off with them.

She doesn't, though. She sets them down on the sidewalk and sits down, ready for the show.

You go to join her.

Rickety lights the lighter, then uses the flame to light the fountain, and then he and your mom run towards you as the fuse lights up.

A moment later, a great shower of sparks shoots up from the cone, making a beautiful pattern of lights against the darkening sky.

You watch in fascination as gold and red

sparks shoot into the air.

"Wow," says Rackety. "I guess it doesn't matter how old it is. It worked just fine."

"I dunno," says Rickety. "It seems kind of small."

"It's not small." You point at how high the sparks are flying. "It's huge."

The look Rickety gives you says he's seen much bigger fireworks. "There are ones that fly up into the air and explode with loud bangs."

"Be quiet," Rackety orders him.

The sparks continue to spout into the air, then fall to the ground where they glow for a moment and then wink out.

You have never seen anything quite like this before.

Rickety, though, is bored. He is playing with a pebble and barely even looks at the fountain. "I still say it's small."

You're pretty sure it's shooting sparks the full ten feet the label promised.

Then it happens. The wind picks up, knocking the fountain over.

Well, that isn't a problem, because the fountain is more than ten feet away, right?

Wrong. The sparks come shooting at you, and the wind catches them, carrying them along.

Only then does it occur to you that you're sitting right next to a box of fireworks.

"Run!" you shout.

The five of you scatter—you and the raccoons go one direction, and your parents in the other just as a large spark lands in the box of fireworks.

Nothing happens.

You let out a sigh of relief.

Your father holds up a hand and shouts,

"Stay away! Just to be safe."

No sooner are the words out of his mouth than the box of fireworks explodes into a great mass of sparks and fizzles, whistles and bangs, lighting up the houses around you and blinding you for a moment.

"Oh, wow..." says Rickety. "Now that's more like it."

The grass nearby has caught fire, though, and there's no water to put it out. Nor can you run over and stomp on the flames, because more fireworks might ignite at any minute.

Your father pulls out his cellphone and calls the fire department. They're no doubt tired of hearing from your family by now.

You made a lot of good decisions here, but some bad things still happened. Fireworks are tricky, so let's look at what you learned.

1. You chose a place that was away from all the houses and dry grass to light the fireworks, and that was very smart. Always light fireworks far away from anything that can catch fire.

2. You read the label on the firework and figured out how far it can shoot sparks. That is also very good. One thing to remember, though, is that it is harder to shoot sparks straight up than any other direction. Sparks flying up get pulled down by gravity. Sparks shooting sideways, after the fountain fell over, can go a lot further, so always remember that

and make sure to give a firework like this extra space.

3.	You didn't have water nearby, and that is a very bad thing. Even if you're setting off fireworks in a safe place, you must have a bucket of water in case of fires. You also want to soak the used fireworks in it for a good long while before throwing them away.

4.	Rackety carried the other fireworks away from the one you were lighting. Always, always keep the other, unlit fireworks away from ones you're lighting.

5.	You all sat around the box of fireworks, and you don't want to do that. Just in case a stray spark lands in the box of fireworks, sit somewhere away from the box.

6. You lit a firework that was old and learned that even old fireworks can still work correctly. As long as they are stored in a dry place, fireworks can last a long time. Here's the thing, though: Your city or country may have laws against storing fireworks for longer than a certain amount of time. Make sure if you have leftover fireworks that your adults know how long they can keep them. And remember, while they are being stored, you want to avoid anything that might light them on accident. In your fire evacuation plan, make sure to avoid anywhere in your house that your family might have stored fireworks.

There are four endings to this story, though, and each one will teach you different things about fireworks. If you haven't read all four, you can...

...go back one step and choose to light the bottle rocket instead (turn to page 40),

go back two steps and choose to light fireworks on your own street (turn to page 10),

go back to the beginning and re-read the first scene (turn to page 3), or

if you've read all four endings, turn to page 58 for a last message from Rickety and Rackety.

RICKETY AND RACKETY SAY GOODBYE

That night, as you're getting ready for bed, you hear a familiar scratch on your window. Two furry, masked faces peer in at you.

The raccoons aren't allowed in your house, but you can open the window to talk to them, so you do.

"We're here to say goodbye," says Rackety.

"What?" you ask.

"Winter's coming soon," says Rickety. "And we need to get fat."

"Oh... to hibernate?"

"Well." Rickety draws herself up to her full height. "We are not true hibernators. We can be active year-round. But winter is cold and it's nice to be able to sleep a lot."

"We really liked the forest when you went camping," says Rickety. "So we're going to go back there for the winter."

"But it's dangerous," you argue. "There are bears and wolves and coyotes and stuff."

"Eh, don't worry about that," says Rickety. "We know how to take care of ourselves. When the weather's warm, we may come back into the city. We don't know."

"But I'll miss you," you say.

"We'll miss you, too," says Rickety. "You

have to promise not to get any bigger over the winter, or we might not recognize you."

"What?" You look down at yourself. "I can't stop growing, guys. It doesn't work that way."

"No?" says Rickety. "Oh well, it was worth asking."

"We won't actually not recognize you," Rackety assures you. "You'll smell the same."

"The fire department is putting out traps for us," says Rickety. "It's time to disappear for a while."

You really don't want to say goodbye.

Rackety reaches in and pats your face with her paw. "You know we never really go anywhere, right? Not while you have our books to read. We'll always be right here."

"Setting stuff on fire," Rickety adds. He pats you on the face as well.

Then both of them turn and hop down from your windowsill and scamper off into the night.

We hope you've enjoyed the Rickety and Rackety adventures, and that you learned from them. (We're not sure if Rickety and Rackety did...) You can get all of their lessons in *Rickety and Rackety: The Complete Fire Unsafety Collection.*

GET FREE BOOKS!

When you sign up for our mailing list at littlebooksofBIGchoices.com, you will receive the first book of every series we write for free. Head on over and sign up today!

littlebooksofBIGchoices.com

ABOUT THE AUTHOR

D.Z. Mah is science fiction and fantasy author, Emily Mah (who also writes contemporary fiction as E.M. Tippetts), and her two young sons. While stuck at home during the 2020 pandemic, they started to get bored and so made up some very silly stories to keep themselves entertained. They hope you are also entertained by the menagerie of mythical creatures and motley crew of characters who brightened their days during a dark time.

Printed in Great Britain
by Amazon

68877772R00043